THE
FROG
ON
ROBERT'S
HEAD

by David Cleveland
pictures by Lisa Campbell Ernst

COWARD, McCANN & GEOGHEGAN, INC. · NEW YORK

Text copyright © 1981 by David Cleveland
Illustrations copyright © 1981 by Lisa Campbell Ernst
All rights reserved. This book, or parts thereof,
may not be reproduced in any form without permission
in writing from the publishers. Published simultaneously
in Canada by Academic Press Canada Limited, Toronto.

Library of Congress Cataloging in Publication Data
Cleveland, David
    The frog on Robert's head.
    Summary: Robert's sister helps him rid himself of a
bored frog who wants to live a boy's exciting life.
    [1. Frogs—Fiction] I. Ernst, Lisa Campbell. II. Ti-
tle.
PZ7.C5986Fr   [E]   81-104
ISBN 0-698-20512-X   AACR2

Printed in the United States of America

To Peg and Hugh
DC

One morning a big green frog jumped on Robert's head and wouldn't get off.

Robert tried to pull the frog off, but it just stretched like rubber and wouldn't let go. He yelled "Get off, frog!" and waved his hands at it, but the frog just waved back.

He tried spinning around very fast, but the frog liked that. It grinned and stuck tight, while Robert only made himself quite dizzy. He hung upside-down from a tree, but the frog loved that. It giggled and swung from Robert's ears.

Finally, Robert gave up spinning, shaking, hanging, rolling, and cartwheeling, and went inside to get some help. His mother was in the kitchen stuffing a pumpkin with tuna fish for dinner.

"Ma! Ma! I got a frog stuck on my head!" Robert yelled.

"That's nice, darling," she said, hardly glancing up. "You have a lively imagination."

"But Ma!" cried Robert, "can't you *see* it?"

"No, dear," she said. "I'd like to play with you, but I'm very busy now. I have to make lemon sauce for the potatoes. Why don't you go show your father."

Robert ran down the hall past his Uncle Chester's room, with the frog's big feet flapping against his forehead. Uncle Chester was there, admiring his huge collection of empty mayonnaise jars.

"Uncle Chester! Uncle Chester! Help! I've got a frog stuck on my head!"

Uncle Chester looked at him and started to chuckle. "What frog?" he snorted.

"It's big and green and it won't come off!" Robert added, pointing at his head.

Uncle Chester began to laugh. "What a kidder you are!" Uncle Chester gasped between laughs. "What a comedian!"

"But don't you *see* it?" cried Robert. At that, Uncle Chester laughed so hard that he popped a button on his trousers and had to run into the closet before he lost his pants.

"Why don't you show your father," he wheezed from the closet.

Robert fled into the backyard. There he found his great big older brother, Bruno. Bruno was having fun trying to smash bricks in half with his baseball bat.

"Bruno," said Robert, "I've got a big frog on my head and he won't get off! Can you see him?" Bruno looked at Robert dully.

"Nah," growled Bruno. "I don't see nuthing. But do ya want me to try and clobber it with my baseball bat?" Robert glanced up at the frog. Then he looked carefully at Bruno with his bat.

"Er, no thanks, Bruno," Robert said.

"Why don't ya go show Pa," Bruno suggested, smashing down on a brick.

This was *awful!* Not only did Robert have a frog on his head, but the frog was invisible to everyone but him! He decided he had to tell his father.

On his way to find his father, Robert passed
his little sister, Charlotte, playing in the sand-
box. He almost stopped to ask her for help, but
decided against it. She was so young. He'd bet-
ter find his father instead. As Robert walked on
by, Charlotte wondered why he was wearing that
frog on his head. Oh, well, she shrugged. Broth-
ers were strange.

Robert's father was in the garage working on his hobby. He was building a cuckoo clock entirely out of peach pits, gluing them together one by one. It was very difficult work, and Robert hated to bother him. But this was an emergency.

"Dad," he called softly.

"What do you want, Robert?" asked his father, as he began to glue the peach-pit cuckoo on its peach-pit perch.

"Dad, I've got a big green frog stuck on my head and he won't come off," said Robert. "And he's invisible," he added. Just then Robert's father dropped the peach-pit cuckoo off its peach-pit perch. Its little peach-pit beak broke into little peach-pit bits. He was furious!

"ROBERT!" his father screeched. "See what you made me do! I've no time for your foolishness! An invisible frog! Can't you see I'm busy?"

"Rrrrrrribbet," croaked the frog.

"WHAT DID YOU SAY?" yelled his father.

"Nothing, Dad," said Robert quietly, and he slipped out of the garage, trying very hard not to step on any cuckoo parts.

What a pickle he was
in! Here he was with a
frog stuck on his head,
and no one else even
believed it was there! He
was going to have to solve
this problem all by
himself.

He tried walking under a low tree branch. At
the last minute the frog covered Robert's eyes
with its flipper feet and Robert whacked his forehead on the branch.

He tried taking a very hot shower, but the frog
just borrowed the soap and lathered up, too.

Robert spent one whole day sitting in a gar-
bage dump so the frog would jump off to eat
flies. But the frog had an ice cream cone instead.

Robert went into his father's closet to disguise himself so the frog wouldn't recognize him. When he came out, the frog was wearing sunglasses and a bow tie.

Finally, Robert gave up. He decided that the frog was here to stay, and that he'd just have to ignore it. But the frog was impossible to ignore.

It sat there on his head during dinner and pushed his arm when he ate, so Robert got gravy on his nose.

"Robert, stop playing with your food," ordered his father.

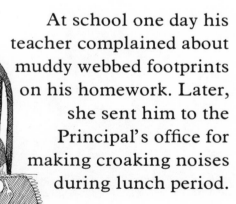

At school one day his teacher complained about muddy webbed footprints on his homework. Later, she sent him to the Principal's office for making croaking noises during lunch period.

Robert didn't know what to do about that frog. He sat on the curb after school with his head in his hands.

"Why me?" he asked out loud, "WHY ME?"

"Because you're a lot of fun," said the frog.

"You *talk!*" gasped Robert.

"Sure," replied the frog, "doesn't every invisible frog?"

"But why are you sitting on my head? What do you want? What can I do to get you off?" Robert was very excited.

"Hey, calm down, kid," said the frog, leaning back and getting comfortable. "Relax. One question at a time."

"Why are you on my head?" Robert demanded. The frog just smiled. Finally he said:

"Well, you see, I thought it was *dull* being a frog. It looked like much more fun being a boy, so I decided to try a boy's life for awhile."

"What do you mean by *awhile?* How long do you plan to stay up there?" Robert asked.

"I don't know," answered the frog. "I've really only begun to see what boys do. I'll probably hang around until I get the whole picture."

Robert thought hard. If he didn't do something, this frog might stay on his head for years!

"Look," Robert said, "I'll make a deal with you. It could be months before you see everything a boy does. But if, in the next two weeks, I show you everything I can think of, will you promise to leave at the end of that time?"

"It's a deal, kid," said the frog.

So, in the next two weeks Robert did some *very* odd things, or so they seemed to the people who couldn't see the frog on his head:

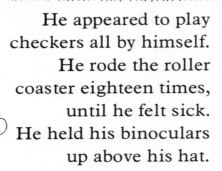

He appeared to play checkers all by himself. He rode the roller coaster eighteen times, until he felt sick. He held his binoculars up above his hat.

He went sledding even though there wasn't any snow.

He cut the top off his football helmet.
He took pictures of himself with his camera.
He always asked for TALL desserts.
He only read the bottom halves
of comic books.
He slept sitting up in bed.
He built a tiny extra room
on the top of his treehouse.

He skated. He ran. He built forts. He balanced
on the tops of fences. He played hide-and-seek,
baseball, basketball, tetherball, hockey, soccer,
and even leapfrog! He ate pizza, hot dogs, cotton
candy, and ice cream. He traded marbles, pulled
pigtails, rang doorbells, blew bubbles, and hung
around the corner doing nothing. He even
cleaned his room. Once.

In two weeks Robert managed to do everything he would normally do in a whole year. His parents were concerned, and the neighbors were starting to wonder. Each night he fell into bed totally exhausted, but all he could say was: "Just a few more days, a few more days."

At last the two weeks were up.
"I've shown you
everything I do," said
Robert to the frog. "Now
you must get off
my head."
"Sorry, kid," said the
frog. "These have been
the best two weeks of my
life. I'm *never* coming
down. I love
being a boy!"
"But you promised!
YOU PROMISED!"
cried Robert.
"I had my flippers
crossed," lied the frog.

Robert was speechless. He walked slowly up
to his room and sat down on his bed, just staring
at the floor.

Just then there was a
soft knock on his door,
and in walked his little
sister, Charlotte.

"What do you want?"
he asked, sulking.

"How come you keep
that dumb-looking frog
on your head, Robert?"
she asked him.

"Charlotte!" said
Robert, jumping up. "Can
you *see* the frog?"

"Of course I can, silly,"
she said. "Why are you
keeping that ugly thing
up there, anyway?"

"I'm *not* keeping it there," moaned Robert.
"It's *stuck* up there!" He told her everything
about the frog—how he tried to get rid of it, how
it liked being a boy, and how it wouldn't leave.
"What am I going to do?" Robert pleaded.

"That's *easy*," said Charlotte, and she began
to whisper in his ear. The frog tried to listen at
Robert's other ear, but it couldn't hear anything.
Robert's eyes got big, and a wide smile appeared
on his face.

"Of course!" he said. "I'll start first thing in
the morning."

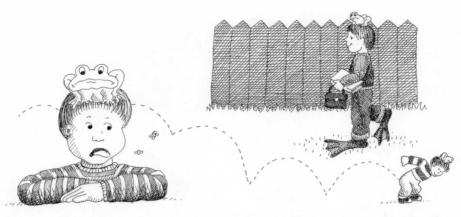

The next day he began behaving very strangely
indeed:

He never walked anywhere. Instead, he
hopped.

He never spoke, except to say "Rrrrrrrribet!"

He wore swim fins to school.

He tried to catch moths with his tongue.
(Luckily, he was too slow.)

He entered frog-jumping contests at county
fairs.

And he spent whole days at the pond, trying
to sit on lily pads, or hiding in water up to his
nose.

He did these things for two whole weeks, even though he knew people were getting worried about him. Finally, the frog couldn't stand it anymore.

"This is dull, *dull, DULL!*" it complained, stamping its webbed foot. "You're acting just like a frog! Are you crazy?"

"Rrrrrrrribet," replied Robert.

"OOOOOOOOH! That does it!" croaked the frog, and with a sound like a cork popping it simply disappeared. Gone. Kaput. Nowhere in sight.

"I'm free! I'm free!" cheered Robert, dashing out of the water and touching the top of his head to be sure. He ran home just as fast as he could to find his sister. She was in the backyard.

"Sis! Sis! Your idea worked! The frog is gone!" he said joyfully.

"Of course, silly," she smiled. "I *told* you all you had to do was act like a frog."

Suddenly there was a huge crash from the garage, and the sound of thousands of falling peach pits. Out of the garage ran Robert's father, speaking wildly and pointing at his head.

"Yow! Help! There's a big green frog on my head! It won't come down!" he yelled. "And it's eating a peach! Quick! Pull it off! Do something! Don't just stand there like dummies!"

Robert and Charlotte looked at the frog hap-
pily smacking on its peach. Then they looked at
their father raging and sputtering at them. Then
they looked at each other . . . and winked.

"What's the matter?" yelled their father. "Can't
you see it? Can't you see it?"

"Gosh, Dad, no," they said. "But did you say
'Rrrrrrrribet'?"